J MAC is the FREESTYLE KING!

Written By: Terri Thomas

Illustrated By: Wendy Sefcik

Inspired by James 'J Mac' Garrett

For my Homie,

**Thank you for seeing in me what I forgot was there and reminding me
to make time for my dreams too. You are the spark that lit the flame.
I dedicate this book to you.**

Pink

Christian,
Keep God First
and Follow your dreams!
Terri Thomas

First published by Dog Ear Publishing
4010 W. 86th Street, Ste H
Indianapolis, IN 46268
www.dogearpublishing.net

ISBN: 978-160844-453-3

This book is printed on acid-free paper.
This book is a work of fiction. Places, events, and situations in this book are purely fictional and any resemblance to actual persons, living or dead, is coincidental.

Printed in the United States of America

This is a story of a boy named J Mac.
He was tall and slim and always had a book in his backpack.

He lived in a town by the name of Conroe
with his Mom and his Dad and his sister Lil Mo.

He also had a dog that was really overweight
because Lil Mo was always feeding him food off her plate.

All the pooch did was eat and eat;
so much so that he could barely stand on his feet.

J Mac had three friends who were very, very close.
These are the boys that he played with the most.

The first one lived around the corner and his name was Benny.
He had big ideas on making money and saved all his pennies.

Number two was Joel – he moved to Conroe from Mexico.
He always carried a camera and took pictures everywhere he would go.

The third was his cousin; they called him Big Cat.
He loved all kinds of cars and dreamed of owning his Dad's big black Cadillac.

J Mac thought school was cool and he liked basketball.
He played everyday with his friends at the park by the mall.

Everyone knew he rarely wore a frown.
He loved new sneakers and his favorite shirt was brown.

He loved music and listened to the radio all day long.
Sometimes with his friends, they would make up a sing-a-long song.

But what J Mac liked to do much more than anything,
was to make up rhymes, he called himself the freestyle king.

Every morning when he woke he would say the same thing.
My name is J Mac and I'm the freestyle king!

He would practice everyday; sometimes from 8 to 8.
He said "practice makes perfect and its how the great become great!"

J Mac would rhyme at every chance he would get;
at school, at the store, even at the vet.

"My name is J Mac and I'm the freestyle king!
Dog's got the blues and he looks so confused.
Doctor, Doctor give me the news!
Does Dog's tummy hurt because he ate my new shoes?"

Oh, how J Mac loved to rhyme!
He would read the dictionary and learn one new word at a time.

It was that one thing; that one skill that gave him so much joy.
But most didn't take him seriously; they called him a silly boy.

"Get out of here with that – your time is up!
How can you be the freestyle king? Did you make that up?"

Most of the kids would laugh and tell jokes.
The only time they would stop was if J Mac was with his folks.

Most people did not believe. Most could not understand.
But J Mac had a goal. He had a grand plan.

He had an idea how to show the kids that were cruel.
So he gathered his friends one day after school.

He said to Benny, Big Cat, Joel and Lil Mo
that he wanted to enter the Conroe Citywide Talent Show.

"What? Huh? Nah, are you for real?"
Their shock and awe they could not conceal.

You see this was not just some little itty bitty talent show.
The whole town came to watch; the whole town of Conroe.

The talent would come from far and wide.
The competition was fierce, many wanted the prize.
Martin with his mind blowing magical tricks;
Mrs. Jenkins with her oodles of dancing poodles,
I think she has 26?

Bart the butcher with his tuba piano drum musical thing;
The Olsen triplets with their beautiful harmonies, boy they could really sing!

How exactly would J Mac
be able to win a thing?

After all, he just *called*
himself the freestyle king.

If that wasn't enough to
make them look at him
funny;

How would they get the
$150 entrance fee money?

J Mac said, "Hold up, wait a minute!
Will you please let me finish?"

Everyone got quiet and patiently waited
as J Mac jumped up, he seemed so elated!

"I think we should make a group. You all can sing
and then I'll come out as the freestyle king!"

"I believe we can make a great sing-a-long song.
I believe we can do it. I know I'm not wrong."

Big Cat looked at J Mac and said, "Even if our sing-a-long song is great;
how do we get the money all I have is $8?"

Lil Mo and Joel, they also chimed in.
Joel had $5.25 and all Lil Mo had was a $10.

Everyone was talking; it got loud all over again,
until J Mac noticed Benny had raised up his hand.

J Mac pursed his lips and let out a piercing whistle.
He didn't do that often because it pierced their ears like a missile.

They stopped shouting and talking, that sound always gave them a scare.
The commotion had stopped and they to saw Benny's hand in the air.

$5.25
$10.00
$8.00
$24.75
+ $42.00
$90.00

Benny cleared his throat and started to speak.
You see Benny knows how to make money. His skills are unique.

"Ok, you three have a total of $23.25.
J Mac, what do you have?"
"24.75"

"That brings up a total of $48. I have $42 and that brings us to $90.
How much do we need? Someone remind me?"

Joel said, "We need a total of $150."
Benny said, "Ok, that leaves a balance of $60."

They were almost there but it wasn't quite enough.
The extra $60 seemed kind of tough.

Benny sat there and he looked all around.
Finally, he looked down on the ground.

He looked up and down and again all around.
He said "I'll be back shortly" and left without another sound.

J Mac and the crew knew Benny was not insane.
Because he had a real gift when the money was funny and the change was strange.

It took 45 minutes for him to come back.
He carried some rakes and some trash bags were hanging out of his back pack.

Benny said, "Ok, I've got it all figured out.
I just talked to our neighbors and they'll help without a doubt."

"I want you to look and see what I see."
Benny looked up and down and walked toward a tree.

"The leaves, they've started to fall.
Lots of trees, lots of leaves, I propose we rake them all."

"I've found six houses. Count 1, 2, 3, 4, 5, 6.
If we rake the leaves and pick up the sticks,
They will pay us $10 each and our problem will be fixed."

Wow! J Mac, Joel, Big Cat and Lil Mo looked so proud.
Benny had figured it out. They gave him a high 5 all the way around.

Now they had even more of a plan.
Everyday after school they would practice their sing-a-long song.
Every Saturday they would clean up the yards until all the leaves were gone.

As long as they worked together their plan would be grand.
They could count on each other to lend a helping hand.

So they raked and they bagged and they sang and J Mac rhymed.
They worked hard every day; so hard they would lose track of time.

So Lil Mo got a calendar and they would cross off the days.
It was three weeks, and then two until it was one day away.

That night before J Mac went to bed,
he got down on his knees and bowed his head like he always did.

He said, "Now I lay me down to sleep.
I pray the Lord my soul to keep.

I ask you God for this favor today.
The Conroe Citywide Talent Show is just one day away.

We've all worked so hard, every single day.
We earned the money and stashed it away.

We got the $150 entrance fee.
We helped our neighbors, we raked all the leaves.

We practiced and practiced our sing-a-long song.
I made a great freestyle. I know it's strong!

I don't want to let down my friends.
They always stand by me until the end.

But you see God there is just one little thing.
Please help me win so I can really be the freestyle king.

I want Lil Mo, Benny, Big Cat and Joel to be proud.
It takes a lot of courage to stand up in front of such a big crowd.

So again God, this means more to me than anything
For me and for them I've got to be the freestyle king!"

So he prayed for his little sister and his Mom and his Dad.
He prayed for his friends that he wouldn't let them down and make them all sad.

He prayed and he prayed for a very long time.
Until his Mom softly tapped his shoulder it was way past his bed time.

His Dad picked him up and gently put him in the bed.
His Mom pulled the covers up snug under his chin.

She kissed his forehead and whispered in his ear,
"No matter what, you're a winner, have no fear."

They turned off the light and J Mac drifted to sleep
dreaming of the competition they would have to beat.

Before he knew it his alarm began to ring.
The day was finally here. They would show everyone he was really the freestyle king.

He leapt out of bed as he heard the birds sing.
As loud as he could he said, "My name is J Mac and I'm the freestyle king!"

So in came Lil Mo. They went downstairs.
Benny, Big Cat and Joel were eating pancakes; they were already there.

The plan for the day was Big Cat's Dad would drive them at noon.
They would ride in the Big Black Cadillac and noon came soon.

So they practiced some more. J Mac rhymed and they sang
all the way to the show, this was not a game.

They got there only to find out they'd go first.
Joel panicked and said, "Man, that's the worst!"

Everyone's stomach felt like butterflies.
You could tell they were nervous from the look in their eyes.

It seemed like forever but it became their time.
J Mac looked at the clock. It was 2:09.

They went out on the stage. The crowd was big and the silence was long.
J Mac looked at his friends and he knew he had to stand strong.
After all, he was the reason that they had come along.

All of a sudden he did an incredible thing.
He opened his mouth and *he started to sing*!

His friends looked for a moment in a state of shock.
But they soon figured it out and the shock wore off.

Benny, Big Cat, Joel and Lil Mo started to sing.
They sang louder and louder. It was an amazing thing!

Then J Mac switched it up and started to flow.
With every word, every rhyme, their confidence would grow.

They were dancing and singing and he was freestyling.
He saw his Mom and his Dad in the crowd and they were smiling!

It was amazing, incredible, a sight to see.
J Mac just knew he would win and be the freestyle king!

When their time was up they had to sit and wait... and wait... and wait to find out their fate.

With each new act, they began to see
awesome talent, especially the Olsen girls time 3.

J Mac started to question with every shout. "Maybe we didn't win?"
He started feeling some doubt.

What would he do if he let his friends down?
Never mind all the kids with their jokes around town.

Finally the talent show had come to an end.
It came to the part when they would find out who would win.

Everyone was quiet. You could hear a pin drop
As the Mayor, Mr. Jones went to the podium and stopped,

He said that there were no losers here today
because to get up in front of everyone was something very brave.

He opened the envelope and called out third place,
Mrs. Jenkins with her oodles of dancing poodles, filling up a lot of stage space.

Next Mayor Jones called out number two.
It was Mario and Mario with their Yodel-ay-hee-hoo!

Now came the moment. This was it.
J Mac and the crew clenched each others fist.

It's time for the winner, number one. . . crown the king!
A drum roll and the Mayor said, "Bart the Butcher and his tuba piano drum
musical thing!"

Oh no! The disappointment, their faces so sad.
J Mac looked at his friends and he felt so bad.
He said, "C'mon, let's go. It's time to meet my Mom and Dad."

So they went outside and as they walked toward the car;
They heard something amazing, even from a far.

An enormous crowd of people stretched from here to there.
They walked a little closer and J Mac and the crew became aware.

They heard the crowd as the crowd started to sing
"Here comes J Mac! He's the freestyle king!"

You see even though they didn't win it was a very brave thing
to get up in front of all those people and rhyme and sing.

So J Mac and his friends won something much more valuable than a prize.
They won respect in so many people's eyes.

He looked at Benny, Big Cat, Joel and Lil Mo
and he knew he had the best friends a boy could know.

He smiled at his friends as they started to sing.
He said it loud; he said it proud,
"My name is J Mac and I AM the freestyle king!"

CPSIA information can be obtained at www.ICGtesting.com
Printed in the USA
LVIW01n2054200817
545738LV00002B/5